George Livingstone Fenton

The Canary

And other Poems

George Livingstone Fenton

The Canary
And other Poems

ISBN/EAN: 9783337398118

Printed in Europe, USA, Canada, Australia, Japan

Cover: Foto ©Andreas Hilbeck / pixelio.de

More available books at **www.hansebooks.com**

THE CANARY

AND

Other Poems

'

BY

GEORGE LIVINGSTONE FENTON M.A.

(LATE CHAPLAIN AT POONA BOMBAY; RECENTLY CHAPLAIN
AT SAN REMO ITALY)

" Yet would I press you to my lips once more,
Ye wild, ye withering flowers of Poesy."
H. KIRKE WHITE

FRANK MURRAY
DERBY LEICESTER AND NOTTINGHAM

LONDON
S. E. STANESBY 180 BROMPTON ROAD S.W.
1891

TO

IDALINE LENORE

.

___

BLESSINGS BE WITH THEE, IDALINE,
FOR THEE THIS LATEST WREATH I TWINE,
SWEET HUMAN LOVE AND LOVE DIVINE.

San Remo 1890

CONTENTS

THE CANARY

BY THE SAME AUTHOR

BLANCHE OR BEHIND THE VEIL.

16mo 24 pp. white cloth gilt

PRINTED FOR PRIVATE CIRCULATION

The few remaining copies may be had price 1/- post
free of

FRANK MURRAY DERBY

THE CANARY.

(Verses partly composed in Sleep)

[EVERY lover of Poetry is familiar with Coleridge's
"*Kubla Khan*," and with the origin of its composi-
tion. Until this morning, I have been a sceptic;
my own experience has convinced me. Reader,
hear my story.]

Last night, or rather early this morning, I seemed to
be sitting—it needs not to specify where or with
whom—in a small room, the half-opened casement
whereof fronted the west. On one side of the
mantel-piece hung a bird-cage. One present
remarked that its tenant looked sulky and ill-at-
ease: whereupon the fair owner, opening the door
of the cage, drew him out and, unregardful of the
open window, placed the Canary upon a Bible
which lay expanded on the table. What followed,
is related in the following lines.

Hitherto is no marvel. But when all was over, the
weeping girl, I dreamed, requested me to put the
incident into rhyme. I instantly complied, and—
methought—composed the lines beneath, as far as
the word "singer." When just about to recite
them to her, my sister called me, and I awoke;
but the verses remained fresh upon the tablets of
memory.

Gently she drew him from the golden cage,
And placed him drooping on the sacred page—
The trembling bird, bewildered, back retired :—
Then, by Isaiah's prophet-notes inspired,
Poured forth a stream of song so wild and shrill,
Awed was each heart, and every tongue was still ! —

1

He paused— from the half opened casement shone
A stream of glory from the setting sun :
Glanced his keen eyes, his downy plume was stirr'd,
Quivered each winglet of the wonderous bird.
Expectant silence sat on every soul ;
Sudden, a low unwonted music stole
From forth his parted beak, while on him fell
That halo from the Heavenly Israel.
" Farewell ! "—for thus articulate the sound
Thro' that admiring audience rolled around :—
" Farewell, sweet girl !—thy favourite hastes to join
" The spirits of his brother-birds divine.
" Yet, when at eve o'er thine enslumbered sense
" Mysterious music breathes its influence,
" Wilt thou not know the singer ? "—

                      As he sings,
A soft air sighs in his dilated wings ;
He rose, and, as the girl stood weeping there,
Passed from her sight, and cleft the ambient air.

WAKING THOUGHTS.

(*Ætat* 16.)

Awaked! awaked! I strive to sleep in vain!
Thought eddying crowds on thought across my brain.
As the waves roll upon the stormy main.

O Promised Land, I lift my soul to thee!—
How slow my bark glides onward thro' the sea
Of life, all void and drearisome to me!

No pilot I her erring course to guide,
While the lost sail-yards float upon the tide,
And the swoln surges beat her shivering side.

O for the Land of Promise! to behold
Isles of the blesséd to mine eyes unrolled,
Their mountains waving with eternal gold!

Hail happy themes of old prophetic strain—
Elysium chanted by the Mantuan swain
Ormuz' glad isle, or Mathra's holy plain.

Celestial Eden—Canaan of the skies—
Leucè whose stream with pearls of Omman vies—
Homes of the pure, the patient and the wise!—

There the first patriarchs of the sons of men,
Throned in perpetual glory, crowd the plain,—
Heaven's palaces with harpings ring again!

Angelic footsteps tread the star-paved ground;
Earth's holiest martyrs, there with honour crowned,
Swell with triumphant voice the pealing sound.

But ha! what mightier form approaches now,
With train of thousands?—Spirit, who art thou?—
What mild majestic radiance girds thy brow?

3

' Tis he—the awful seer whose arm defied
The purple-mantled Pharaoh in his pride,
And stretched his wand, and stemmed the ocean's
    tide !—

Ye, too, are there, whose eagle-eyes of light,
GOD'S elder scripture read by reason right,—
The great Athenian and the Stagirite.

Of every clime, of every creed, and age,
Hebraic rabbi, or Hellenic sage,
Who pored o'er Philo's or o'er Plato's page,—

Brethren in love and faith now met from far,
Glorious they shine : their light is Bethlehem's Star,
The SHILOH, LOGOS, and the AVATAR !

    PENRITH.

A NURSERY SCENE*.

It was a half-angelic sight,
  A young and lovely girl caressing
With taper fingers lily-white,
  And softly to her bosom pressing
A bird of golden plumage bright,
While nestling to its nurse's breast,
Delighted to be thus caress'd.
With panting heart and closéd wing
It lay in feignéd slumbering :
And near beside that gentle maid,
A younger urchin blithely played,
And throwing back his fair hair's cluster
From off his brow of whitest lustre,
Half-playfully, half-chidingly,
Peep'd in her face imploringly,
With all an infant's wile, that she
Would in his artless gambols join,
And round his top the whip-cord twine.

T'was a glad sight might well supply
The Bard, (alas! no Bard am I,)
With divinest imagery :
For seem'd not that young graceful creature,
  The *girl* upon whose brow nor Time,
  Nor pining sorrow yet, nor crime,
Had dared to write one strange defeature ;
That bird which better than the wit
Of cunning'st artist e'er could hit,
Would counterfeit to human sense
    The sleep of baby innocence ;
And that small blue-eyed fairy boy,
Aye-prattling with some pretty toy :—
Seem'd they not there,—(nor idly deem
Such thought the poet's phrenzied dream,)
Meet emblems of the Heavenly Three,
Gay Hope, meek Faith, kind Charity !

---

*The three Canaries, versified were in no way related

5

" What ails thee, plaything, that no more
" Thou sleepest calmly as of yore ?
" Awhile, my little bird be free,
" Go sing the song of Liberty !"
She said, and with obedience true
Forth from her hand the prisoner flew,
And round and round with fluttering wing
    In circling flight it traced the room,—
Poor, timid, harmless, happy thing,
    Unmindful of the coming doom !
Now perching on Eliza's chair,
Now lightly skimming o'er her hair,
The willing captive seemed to grieve
A moment his dear nurse to leave ;
Now quiet resting on the ground
It watched the top spin lightly round.

Tired of his sport, the fickle child,
Or by some fairer toy beguiled,
Bounds o'er the floor with laughter wild,
Nor heeds his small companion there :—
" Stay, LIVINGSTONE, the Bird beware ! "
Ah me ! too late the warning came !
Lo, tears of anguish and of shame
Are streaming from the Murderer's eyes !
    No words of blame Eliza said,
    But bending on the ground her head,
With broken accents, tears and sighs,
    Scarce could she deem her favourite dead.

HYMN TO THE OMNIPRESENT DEITY.

Where Nilus' holy stream
Reflects pale Isis' beam ;—
Where the groves o'erhung with palm,
    Graceful wave their odorous boughs,
And the valleys breathing balm
    Are scented with their pale sweet rose ;
Where, as the weeping willows cast
    Their shadows o'er the spray,
The Nile-goose bathes her downy breast,
    To shun the scorching ray ;
Where the silver lotus blows,—
Where the red flamingo glows,—
There, O God, Thy voice is heard,
There Thine awful name revered !—

Where the desert-waste expands,
Where burn Sahara's fiery sands,
Where the wandering Arab's dart
Poisonous wounds the flying hart,
And, springing from the thickets deep,
Tigers rouse him from his sleep ;
Where the ocean's sullen roar
Thunders round Columbia's shore ;
Where snowy flakes the whirlwinds bear,
Rushing through the Lapland air,
While o'er the water's icy edge
Tinkling dashes the rapid sledge,
As lakes and rocks and mountains high
Like magic vanish from the eye,
And on the startled stranger rings
The rushing by of fearful things,
The dogs' low melancholy cry,
The ice-cliffs crumbling heavily :—
There—even there—Thy Presence fills
Lap's frozen plains and Greenland's forky hills

7

Where the sacred Ganges rolls,
And cocoas swell their milky bowls,
Where the fragrant almond's shade
Or cool bananas bless the glade ;
Where Albion's exiled children view
The shadow of the cloudless blue
   Sleeping on an Indian river :
Faëry forms are blooming there,
Young birds glancing thro' the air,
   Starry insects twinkling ever
   Thro' the wood-gloom dance and quiver ;—

Her spices where old Ceylon flings,
Or Greece her olive-harvest sings,—
Where Afric yields her palmy wine,
Or Gallia plucks her clustering vine,—
Where with rich grain the valleys smile
In western Albion's happy isle,—
Still while to Thee my thoughts I raise,
My bosom swells with grateful praise
Earth's brightest beauties disappear,
And God, my God, alone inhabits there !

THE GARDEN OF EDEN.

Lovely was Eve on Eden's glorious plain,
When of the drooping flowers she wove a chain,
And gaily flung the wreath around the lion's mane,

Or with light footsteps down the sloping brow
Measured her swiftness with the panting doe,
That bounded by her side like arrow from the bow.

Fair Protoplast of fairest womanhood !
Sweet help and solace of man's varying mood,
Blest by her Maker's word with emphasis of " good !"

Then each fresh view yet more her soul amazed,
And warm with gratitude and love she gazed
On all the beauteous scene, and her Creator praised,

For each fair flower that courts the balmy air,
All shrubs that choicest leaves or odours bear,
Or on whose laden boughs the mellow fruits appear :—

The tall palmetto—Persia's lonely pride,
The forest oak that with the cedar vied,
All music-haunted groves graced Eden's sylvan side.

The cypress in dark shadowing grandeur towers,
And, interwoven with the citron bowers,
The pensile grape its green and purple clusters
showers.

While, round her gamboling, snuffed each rare
perfume,
Or drank the brooks, or spread the rainbow-plume,
All that the sun's bright beams with life and health
illume.

9

There might she see in amity recline
Fire-eyed hyænas with the milk-white kine,
Or round the panther's neck his folds the snake
    entwine.

Dark bristled boars with wolves and lambkins played,
Soft on her lap his paw the lion laid,
Or, low his regal brow bending, meek homage paid.

At her approach beside the reedy flood,
Bowing his vasty bulk Behemoth stood,
Behemoth "made for man," "chief of the ways of
    God!"*

No wintry winds the grove's dark foliage shook,
No nightly frost congealed the purling brook,
Nor its dumb swimmers yet had felt the treacherous
    hook.

No toiling merchant urged the camel's speed
No barbarous rider gored his foaming steed
Nor yet the murderous knife bade the mute sufferer
    bleed.

Many a fair spirit then on trembling wing
Hovered o'er Eden's bowers, listening
While rose the hymn of praise to men and angels'
    King.

But clouds veil o'er the azure hues of heaven ;
Despair's grim car thro' Pleasure's lawn is driven ;
Trembles the guarded Mount, blasted and tempest-
    riven !

The Tree of Life is scorched by human tears ;
The yew its melancholy head uprears,
And with its dank shade all the under-grasses seres.

Hark, a wild wailing cry ! with glaring eyes
The leopard springs his victim to surprise ;
The bleeding dam amid her mangled offspring dies.

The wolf his hunger strives to sate in vain,
Their rugged tusks the bristled wild-boars strain,
The angry lion growls exulting o'er the slain.

Rancour and hate, and strife to madness swell,
Nought can the rage of savage discord quell,
Man strikes at kindred man mid the loud battle's yell !

---

*Job xl. 15—19.

Voice of a brother's blood is on the breeze !
Ah ! what avail, O EVE, thy tears to ease
Remorse's baneful pangs, or Death's last agonies !

Hushed are the vales that heard the voice of God ;
Dark are the hills that with His presence glowed ;
One song is left to man—the song of *Ichabod !*

Hark, a " new song !" —above the warbled wail
A voice of mercy floats upon the gale :—
Hail ! sinless child of Eve ! predicted Saviour hail !

Your rapid course, appointed ages, run !
Bard of the earth ! thou too, thy task well done,
Shalt share the high-sphered Milton's wreath in PARA-
DISE RE-WON.

THE SAVIOUR SLEEPING.

Messiah sleeps :—ye blooming flowers of earth,
  Blush into beauty from your leafy bed !
  Ye palms, wave gently o'er His sacred head !

Messiah sleeps :—creatures of finite birth,
  That tread this lower world, or skim the air,
  In silent awe His peaceful slumbers share ;

Your rustling wings, celestial Seraphs, bind !—
  Lash not thy hollow shore thro' all thy deeps,
  Earth-circling Ocean ! thy Creator sleeps !

Hush, ye wild rivers ! and thou aëry wind,
  Within thy rude tumultuous caverns rest !
  Calm thy fierce tempests in an hour so blest !

Or sometimes in low tremulous murmurs rise,
  Breathing sweet incense thro' the cooling shade,
  Where in soft sleep the Prince of Peace is laid.

Yes, slumber sits on Jesus' wearied eyes,
  Yet, lingering on His face, a smile divine
  Still beams with love to man and grace benign.

Emmanuel sleeps :—But Oh ! what mortal ken
  Those dread mysterious visions may behold,
  To the Redeemer in that hour unrolled ?

The hour is come! –Beautiful among men,
  How art thou pierced !—upon that brow divine
  Accursed hands the bloody garland twine.

O Thou Unsearchable, who reign'st above,
  Hast *Thou* forsaken Him ? To Thee He cries,
  " My God ! my God !"—then bows his head, and
    dies.

Tremble, thou earth! Judea's forests bow!
  Arnon and Herman, cloud-capped Lebanon,
  And rocky Nebo, bend their lofty crown!

Souls of the sainted dead, awake!—and thou,
  Glory of Salem, Israel's awful fane,
  Be rent thy mystery-covering veil in twain!—

Past is that hour of woe:—a smile of love,
  And more than angel radiance on His face,
  Ineffably serene, His features grace.

The pangs of Calvary are o'er : Behold!
  Redemption's star gleams bright o'er land and sea,
  And all earth's kingdoms bend the adoring knee.

See, He has risen!—eternal gates unfold!
  From star to fulgent star, aërial powers,
  Sound hallelujahs thro' your silver bowers!—

My harp, in soft sounds hail the glorious morn!—
  Swells from the glass-sea shore the seraph's strain,
  "Glory to God on high, peace and good-will to
    men!"

For heaven's bright crown exchanged the wreath of
    thorn,
  High jubilee the Lamb of Zion keeps!
  But hush, ye wild strings, hush! *Messiah Sleeps!*

Seven-hilled City, hear my word!—
By thy fratricidal lord—
By thy blood-cemented walls—
By each frantic shriek that calls
Thro' Sabine city, vale, or grove,
For the daughter, wife, or love,—
By broken faith and female wrong
Hear the burden of my song—
       Repent thee, Rome!

By the base Tarquinian line—
By the bride of Collatine—
By the desert stream which flows
Where once the towers of Carthage rose—
By each spoiled Corinthian fane—
By the plundered realms of Spain—
By Sylla's and by Cæsar's name,
Each damned to an eternal fame—
       Repent thee, Rome!

By the trammelled nations' cry—
By Judah's walls in dust that lie—
By western Gallia's warrior-train
On their native mountain slain—
By Britannia's sea-beat shore—
By Mona, dyed with Druid gore—
By the sword, the stake, the chain—
By the tortured Christians' pain—
       Repent thee, Rome!

" What! shall a poet blame the earth
" Which gave to glorious Maro birth?
" His lyre where learn'd Lucretius strung,
" Where laughing Horace loved and sung,
" Where Lucan "—
       Thank thee for the name!

It fires anew the indignant flame :
By that foul Prince (it bids me cry)
Who quenched the song of *Pharsaly*,
And by the martyred minstrel's death—
By Seneca's expiring breath—
By those who worshipped in the dust
The altar of imperial lust—
           Repent thee, Rome !—

But ha! a Proteus form art thou—
MYSTERY writ upon thy brow ;—
MAN OF SIN, who sit'st on high,
And lift'st thy lewdness to the sky,
With thy triple crown on pate,
Holding Christ and Christ's in hate,
Prophet false, with fury fired,
Wolf, in sheep-like garb attired,
Serpent, shaped like angel bright,
Satan, counterfeiting light—
           Repent thee, Rome !

By the Albigensian war—
By the blood of brave La Vaur—
By Piedmont's hills in slaughter dyed—
By thy lying, lust, and pride—
By each deed of darkness hid
In Goa or Valladolid—
By Italia's sunlit clime
Cursed with heresy and crime—
By Savonarola's blood
Whose pile illumed the Arno's flood—
By English Hooper's dying groan,—
Thou ANTITYPE OF BABYLON.—
           Repent ! Repent thee, Rome !

VOLTERRÆ: A SONNET.

Volterræ's walls are sunk, her people pale,
  And wild and dreary spread the lone *Maremme*,
Where Macchi's oaks their fallen sires bewail,
  And the sad cypress weeps o'er Arno's stream ;
And save where o'er Volterræ's roofless fanes
  The grey-barked olive hangs her mourning veil,
No sign of life or nature's power remains,
  But dire malaria taints the infected gale.
And thou, too, Rome !—a few short seasons o'er,—
  Bowed by the weight of ages and of fame,
Shalt stand in melancholy pride no more,
  Leaving nought else but an eternal name :
Partaker of thy sons' time-hallowed grave,
Thy dirge, the Desert's voice—thy shroud, old Tiber's
    wave !

SHALL I LAMENT ?

" Shall I lament for FAME ?"
  Hath not the coffin's lid
  The boast of ages hid ?
  Who built the Pyramid,
To èternize his name ?
Where stood Cambyses' tent ?—
No, not for Fame lament !

" Shall I lament for WEALTH ?"—
  Can honour, truth, be sold ?
  May hearts be bought for gold ?
  Yon palsied wretch behold
Who hoards his heaps in stealth,
All wrinkled, wan, and bent !—
Who would for Wealth lament ?

" Shall I lament for PLEASURE ?—
  " The dance, the song, the jest,
  " The purple-tinctured vest,
  " The wine-cup's sparkling zest ? "—
Life's fleeting moments measure,
Recalled as soon as lent !
Nor dance, nor cup lament !

" Shall I lament for SONG ?"
  Sweet tho' the minstrel sing,
  His heart is withering:
  A solitary thing
He walks amid the throng,
With silent anguish spent.
O, not for Song lament !

" Shall I lament for LOVE ?
  " For Beauty's witching smile ?"—
  Beware of Beauty's wile !
  She flatters to beguile.
Go, set thy heart above !—
Repent, repent, repent
Thy days of youth mis-spent !
Thy wasted days lament!

MY BIRTHDAY : A SONNET.

They say, who far to other lands have gone,
  It is a sight most mournful to behold
  The ruins of high cities famed of old—
Palmyra, Baalbec, or of Babylon,—
Colossal skeletons of human pride,
Or tombs of mighty kings now throwing wide
  To every passing wind their royal dust.
There is a melancholy more profound,—
  A grief, methinks, more settled and more just,
When the soul wanders pensively around
  The ruin and the wreck of its own vows,—
How high ! how holy ! and, alas, how vain !
  Spirit of Power, my slumbering spirit rouse
Build the waste places of this heart again !

THE STAR OF DESTINY.

A lone lovely Child—pale, fearless, and wild—
  His gold hair waved bright to the blast:
On his Destiny's Star, as it gleamed from afar,
  His dark eyes were enquiringly cast.

He breathed a low vow—on his eloquent brow
  Sat enthroned all the beauty of Truth:
And methought, may no tear dim thy glorious career,
  No sin blight the flower of thy youth!

"Thou Planet, unroll thy mystical scroll!"—
  Thus dauntlessly questioned the Boy :—
The Star set in gloom—'twas a terrible doom
  For a spirit all radiance and joy !

But the pale Queen of Night poured her silvery light
  Re-illuming earth, ocean, and sky ;
Then he cried out with glee, " There's a Mightier, I see,
  Who is LORD too of Destiny."

THE SEA-WEED.

The Sea-weed, sapling of a grove
  Inviolate to human tread,
In whose dark shades wild monsters rove,—
Sprung from a soil no tiller ploughs,
  Its birth-place among coral cells,
Where genii harbour in its boughs
  And gently wake their sweet-lipped shells,—
  Will twine its wreaths around the dead,
Sole mourner o'er the lonely grave
Where sleep the lovely and the brave.

But sometime on the wave-worn strand
Flung by the giant surge's hand,
Fine as the web Arachne wove,
The summer's scorching heat to prove,
  'Twill weep, like the low violet
By some rude boy in idle play
Snatch'd from the·elm's bare root away :—
  Faint emblems of Man's wayward fate !

THE FADING ROSE.

I deem not that yon withering Rose
Fades everlastingly ;
Again in fairer climes it blows
With sweeter fragrancy.

Some spirit with the flower alighted,
To cheer our wintry gloom,
But earthly guilt and grief have blighted
Its sympathising bloom.

And soon the frail exotic closes
Its petals with a sigh,—
Sighs for its native land, where roses
Wear hues that never die !

And where are they, the gentle ones,
Whom we have loved on earth,
They of kind feelings, looks, and tones.—
Have *they* no second birth ?

Roam they the land of Faëry,
In robes of emerald green ?
Push they their star-skiffs cheerily
Athwart the blue serene ?

Lingers not yet the spirit near,
Where the cold corse low lieth ?
Doth not the Disembodied hear,
Where the lonely-hearted sigheth ?

Surely, sweet tones have beguiled my way,
That never in dream had birth,—
Voices of those who have passed away
Long years from this middle earth.

Sounds not the sweep of their spirit-wings
On the sighing gales of even ?
Have I not heard their elfin strings
Thrill with the notes of Heaven ?

Shades of the Dead ! ye are round me now !
I own your awful spell :
By this quicken'd pulse, and this burning brow,
I know your presence well !

I have seen a shape which I may not tell
Thro' the dim mists of distance gleam,
And a deeper spell on my spirit fell
Than ever in midnight dream.

Stay, soul of the sinless, stay awhile !
Phantom of beauty linger !—
Thou art gone :—but the look, and the tone,
    and the smile
Are left with the lonely singer.

Beautiful Night ! o'er the reposing world
Thou, like a mother o'er her cradled babe,
Draw'st, with still hand, the downy folds of peace.—
O, who can gaze, at midnight's solemn hour,
Upon the star-lit circlet of the skies,
But his heart heaves with an unearthly awe,
Thrilled with a nameless yet o'er-mastering spell ?—
Deep awe, soft sadness, exquisite delight,
O'er my rapt soul their magic charms diffuse !—
Here, then, alone in this sequestered glen,
While the wind's hollow wailings all are hushed,
And hushed the warbling of the woods,—no sound
Save the low gurglings of the rippling brook,
Mournful, yet soothing as the faery tone
Of whispers breathing music to the soul
So soft as if they feared to break the spell
That binds the fond heart of the listening bride:—
Here, while along the dark cerulean heavens
A thousand orbs shed lustre as they roll,
Even while I gaze, the rushing tide of Love,
Voiceless, and tongueless, rolls upon my soul,
My spirit drinks from the immortal fount
Of Poesy, and with a deep serene
Of joy, my GOD ! I thank Thee that *I am*.

Hail, thoughts seraphic, visions glorified
Of heaven-born Poesy ! whose magic spells,
Pure, sweet, ethereal, breathed upon my soul—
Like scents and sounds from some bright spiritual
    world
Hung in its mystery between earth and heaven,—
Thrill and enchant !—O be it mine to pour
A wild and melancholy beauty round,
Wafting the murmurs of mellifluous song
Sweet as the breath of rose-crowned Zephyrus,
Not uninspired : or with a reed of light

To paint the unreal forms of phantasy
From human apprehension thinly veiled
In this world's imagery :—then to stoop,
And o'er the verdant plains and fragrant flowers,
Stream-watered glades and forest-haunting rills,
Fair Nature's mightiest works, admiring muse,
And on the azure sky ! O, I could gaze,
With joy sublimed to ecstasy divine,
For ever on the bright brown clouds that shade
The braided heavens, and all the flaming orbs
That hang in glory or in glory roll !
I ask not clashing cymbals, nor the sound
Of woodland instruments, nor solemn peal
Responsive to the chanting voice of praise ;
But in still moonlight, in the noiseless woods,
Far from light voices, and the unholy shouts
Of revelry (in midnight hush how shrill !
How dissonant from holy communing !)
On the calm heavens while here alone I stand
Serenely gazing, that blue silence falls
Deep on my heart, and then my voice breaks forth
In aery syllables, and I would clothe—
Vainly would clothe—my holiest thoughts, as they
Were things of earth, in this world's holiest names,—
Like him who, on Ilyssus' bank reclined,
Of Love and Beauty 'neath the platane's bough,
Harmonious sung,—Beauty, and Love, and Truth.

Hail Beauty in Truth !—thee highest bards have sung,
Thee Plato loved, and in his heart of hearts
SHELLEY—the spiritual bard, whose dreamy mind
Was haunted by glad mysteries, which he clothed
.In splendid syllables as with a robe
Of a most dazzling whiteness—madly yearned
To clasp thy peerless glories, and alas !
Ixion-like,—(who would not weep for *him*
Who wept for *Adonais ?*)—clasped a cloud—
A Phantasm !—
                    And all hail, ye giant hills,
Ye fresh green pastures, and ye heathery glens,
Where oft, entranced by such melodious sounds,
My soul in kindred ecstacy is lost !—

Alas ! that I must leave the woodland haunts,
And balmy groves, and CUMBRIA'S flowery dales !

24

Her brown-spread moors, and shady dingles grey,
And whispering rills with twinkling ripples bright,
Where oft I roamed in childhood's rosy hours,
A laughing boy the bordering flowers among.

Farewell, melodious warblers, whose sweet songs
Of joy and gladness wont to enchant mine ear,
High as ye soared amid the waves of light
That billowed on the aureate deep of Heaven!

Farewell, ye caves, where, when o'er mortal eyes
Sleep shook his downy wing, alone retired
Like Numa in Egeria's hallowed grot,
I lay, and gazed upon the wizard shapes
Of gods and heroes flashing thro' the clouds,
That bowed my being with a dread delight!

Ye hoary-headed oaks, whose giant arms,
Blackened and withered by a thousand storms,
Rise like the columns of some antique fane,
Palmyra of the forest, over-roofed
By the wide arch of heaven!—ye birchen-trees,
Sweet silent nymphs of beauty, whose white stems,
Graceful and glistening with a silvery haze,
And pendulous tresses in the light air swinging,
Wave to the breath of some aerial music
Inaudible to gross mortality!—
Ye time-worn battlements,* whose antique towers,
Tinged by the moon's pale beam, sublimely rise
So dark and silent!—And thou starry vault
So beautiful, from whence my wayward soul
Would catch her inspiration, fare ye well!—

Farewell, ye voices on the fresh breeze sailing!
Ye gentle elves soft tripping o'er the mead!—
Dear happy scenes of early golden days,
A long farewell!—Farewell the pensive strings
Of my long-cherished lyre! I may not list
To your high strains: for other duties call,
And I must turn away, unwillingly,
From your sweet spells: Yet in this heart enshrined
Still shall the dream of CUMBRIA'S breezy hills,
Her sweet romantic vales, and marble lakes,
Breathe on my harp, and falter on my tongue.
        PENRITH.

*The noble ruins of Brougham Castle.

25

THE ABSENT BARD'S LAMENT.

O not for Brahma's spicy groves,
Where light and free the musk-deer roves,
Thro' plantain bowers and balmy meads,
Her sacred stream where Gunga leads,
And every copse is glittering bright
With the quick fire-fly's quivering light,—

O not for Teheran's rosy bowers,
And almond shrubs, whose clustering flowers
Throw, pendant o'er the crystal stream,
Their beautifully-quivering shade,
Where, lovely as the poet's dream,
Sports naiad-like the glowing maid,—

Not for the Isle whose judas-bowers
With roseate blossoms gleam,
Where the cassia hangs her golden flowers
O'er the wild Ribeiro's stream ;
Where the young Madeirense wreathes her raven hair
With the passion-flower's scarlet bloom,
And the selandry swings her white bells on the air
'Neath the green banana's gloom ;—

Not for the land where Lena laves
Grey Legria's aged walls,
And mournfully the night-gust raves
Thro' Vathek's mouldering halls ;
O not for all the gems which shine
·In dark Golconda's richest mine
With bright and dazzling sheen,—
Would I *thee* change, my native bank !
What tho' thy lowly sides be dank,
And clothed with humble green.
Favonius' harp so sweetly strung
Sighs o'er thee with its balmy breath,
And Beauty's hand hath round thee flung
So tastefully her robe of heath,

Whose mingled colours, white and red,
Or blue, with purple streaks bespread,—
Blended like Highland tartan plaid,
Or the rich gorgeous tints that lie
In some autumnal evening's sky,
Or heaven's bespangled bow,—
'Mid the low moss, or grassy blade,
Or taper bracken's taller shade,
Are bathed in such refulgent hues,
As the grey twilight sheds its dews
Upon the hoar hill's brow,
That, as enraptured here I stand,
Methinks some gay and sportive band
Hath sallied forth from Faerie-land,
While " solemn stillness holds the air,"
And heaven is cloudless and serene,
To deck with imagery fair,
From their own realms of joy, a scene
So beautiful, so wild and sweet,
Where mountains, woods, and waters meet,
And myriad birds on every spray
Hymn vespers to departing day.

*　　*　　*　　*　　*　　*

Thus while in happier days she sung
The infant muse attuned her lyre,
And thus VOREDA'S* groves among,
The minstrel waked his notes of fire.

Tho' the chennar-tree groves all beautiful stand,
Where the wild ass scours o'er the pathless sand,
Yet dearer to him was the delicate flower
Of the rose-tree that blooms in his own home-bower ;
And sweeter to him was the music that swells,
Dear Church of his youth, from thy curfew-bells,
Than the echoing sound from the haughty tower
That speaks not of heaven but mortal power.

Shall he flee, then, with joy to the scenes of his child-
hood,
Again over valley and mountain to roam,
To sport as of old thro' the stream-watered wildwood,
Where kind friends would hail the glad wanderer home ?

---

*VOREDA—Roman name for Penrith.

Ah no ! for the smiles that endeared them are o'er
And the eye that beamed brightest would welcome no
    more,
And the dirge that yet floats on the desolate blast
Would but wake the sad heart to remember the past.
Then rest thee, poor pilgrim, thy home is not here,
Where the dark hours are clouded with sorrow and fear.

She is gone—the Beloved—to those gardens so bright,
Where flowers of most exquisite beauty have birth,
For life's troubled waves hath gained rivers of light
And the fulness of Heaven for the shadows of earth!

TO HER WHO IS NOT.

I would not that Time's withering hand had marred
The vernal freshness of that fair young brow,—
That sin had e'er that guileless heart estranged
From its pure saintlike dreams, or sorrow's tears
Dimmed those sweet serious eyes.—O, all too false,
(Thou of the flute-like voice and seraph smile !)
Too cheerless this dull waste of life for thee !
And thou wast happy, who so early pressed
The grave's calm peaceful pillow.—

                Yet 'twas hard,
Most hard, that one so young, so beautiful,
And good, so soon should die,—so soon should close
Her eyes upon the fresh green fields and flowers,
And sunlit hills that skirted the dear vale,
Her innocent childhood's home ; no more to climb
The steep bank in the buoyancy of youth
And happiness,—no more at early dawn
With the young kids to brush the sylvian dew
From her small delicate feet, her golden tresses
Fanned by the blushing gale.

              I might not clasp
Thy dying hand, nor kiss thy fading brow,
And whisper thee farewell :—'twas sad to see
Thy cheek-rose paling 'neath the icy touch
Of Phthisis, but this throbbing heart had burst
(Mine own, mine island-Peri !) to behold
That bright cheek veiled with death s pale livery !—
They told me thou wast dead—that the damp earth
Was thy lone couch, my ISABEL !—and much
They marvelled that I wept not, breathed no sound
Of woe :—alas ! they knew not there are griefs
That mock all human signs !—But from that hour
Earth lost its charms, and all its fairest scenes,—

Like some fantastic dream's half-imaged shapes
Veiling their dim and shadowy loveliness,—
Gleam dark and indistinct :—in stated rounds
The seasons come, and to their viewless home
Unheeded pass : Hope's wind-winged emblem, *Spring* !
All-beauteous as thou art, thy brightest blossoms
Seem withering to decay : and thou, too, *Summer* !
With thy clear silver streams, and gem-like stars
Rolling or quivering in their azure spheres,
Art dimmed to saddest smile :—and I have lived
To mourn the long, long wintry day, and wake
The night-breeze to the melody of woe,
Tuning its hoarse gust to funereal dirge :—
And I have lived to pore with strange delight
On the deserted mound where thou art laid,
And I have wished to lay my aching nead
Ere long on the green sward, with thee to sleep
The sleep of peace.

AN IMAGINED REALITY.

"It was not all a dream."

All in a trance, when day grew late,
Methought I oped the church-yard gate,
   With a tranquil melancholy,
      And a reverence hushed and deep,
   For the very ground is holy
      Where the holy sleep.

With a spirit-thrilling sound,
O'er the swelling heaps around,
   The solemn bell was pealing
      As the mourning train came on,
   And afar the dirge was stealing
      The evening air upon.

Sadly slow they stepped before me,
And a breathless awe came o'er me,
   When I gazed upon the pall,
      And the bearers clad in white,
   Till within the sacred wall
      They vanished from my sight.

In sooth, it was the saddest sight
To see those maidens clad in white,
   All like dew-bent lilies bending
      As they bore along the bier,
   To her last home attending
      The lovely and the dear.

Now they have laid thee in the earth,
The fairest flower of mortal birth,
   And the heavy clod is falling,
      And the earth-worm seeks his prey,
   And the voice of friends is calling
      The weeping train away.

And thou must in the cold grave dwell
Alone, my gentle Isabel!—
    Those lips which lovers longed to press
    Are stiff and pale and chill,
And thy mild blue eyes are lustreless
    Which sternest hearts could thrill.

Thou art gone—they talk of thee no more,
Their thoughts are busied as of yore,
    And eyes that fondest met thee
    Are bright and tearless now:—
But when shall *I* forget thee?—
When I am low as thou!

LINES ON THE DEATH OF THE REV. S. J.
McLEAN, F.T.C.D.

Spirit ! erewhile who dwelt our haunts among,
Now high-enthroned amid the heavenly throng,
Still if thy love may linger here below,
Forgive the tears these streaming eyes o'erflow !—
Maclean ! I know, I know thy sainted spirit,
Hath gone the land of light and love to herit ;
I know, I know thy franchised soul hath fled,
To mingle with the young and holy dead ;
And thou art happy ;—O how happier far
Than we who wage with sin unequal war !—
Yet who could list thy soft persuasive tone,
Who see thee smile, nor weep that thou art gone ?—
O, when the mournful tidings spread around,
How dull and heavy fell the unwelcome sound !
Chilled was each heart and checked each hearer's
    breath,
As whispering sorrow told the tale of death.
For, all did love thee ! Slander's venomed lie,
That passed not others, passed thee harmless by ;
But they who knew thee best and valued most,
How must *they* weep thy worth untimely lost !
How long lament, as o'er thy tomb they bend,
Their "truest-hearted and their tenderest friend !"*

For me, o'er many a buried friend who mourn,
And sigh for those who never shall return,
Henceforth, thro' this life's few and evil years,
Foremost for thee shall flow the unbidden tears,
Foremost to God this fervent prayer ascend—
" FATHER, like *his*, O make my latest end !"

    DUBLIN.

---

*" The best friend that God was ever pleased to bestow upon
him,—the truest hearted, the most single-minded, the most
devoted, and the tenderest." (*See a beautiful obituary of Mr.
McLean by Bishop O'Brien of Ossory, in the "Dublin Record."*)—
T.C.D

Wake, Maid of melancholy Musings, wake !—
Surely thou know'st that, for thy cherished sake,
Love's gay allurements, Pleasure's rosy smiles,
The field where Glory crowns her favourite's toils,—
Yea, tho' reluctant half, the hallowed door
Of Science, and the palm of Ethic lore,
The wreath which girds the classic student's brow,—
All, all have I forsaken ; and wilt thou
But bend on me a cold neglectful eye ?—
I do remember how, in years gone by,
Lone musing o'er some lay of Old Romance,
And half-enslumbered in a dream-like trance,
The live-long day I wasted ; yet even then
I longed to rise above my fellow-men,—
Not on the wheels of Conquest's crimson car,
Not in the whirlwind empery of War,
But rapt on high, sublimer Muse ! with thee
Upon the wings of Sacred Poesy.—

O sacred Poesy ! divinest name
Of all beneath high heaven's resplendent frame !
How few the lips thy hallowed torch hath fired !
How few, since beauteous Nature first inspired
The Morning-stars, and, as their numbers flowed,
Taught—His best gift—to praise the Giver, GOD !
Alas ! and were those young aspirings vain ?
And the fond hopes that flashed athwart my brain,
Unreal meteors ? Will no worthier ray
Of Genius lighten in this frozen clay ?—
Thou who of old didst Crashaw's song inspire,
Well-pleased who heard'st the tones of Henry's lyre,
Wake, Maid of melancholy Musings, wake !
The silence of thy sorrowing slumber break !
Still must the harp of Henry sleep in death ?—
O thou, if ever I have loved to wreathe
His fadeless urn with the fresh hues of Spring,
Aid my weak hand once more that holier harp to string !

34

Thus as I prayed, I heard a voice reply,
Soft as in summer-eve the breezes sigh
In fitful cadence on Æolian lute,—
" Shall sin-stained man the Harp of Heaven pollute?
" No other hand than hand of Innocence,
" And unsoiled Truth, may draw sweet music thence.
" *If such be thine* "—

Then suddenly I saw,
With deep joy tempered to admiring awe,—
Fair as the fairest Houri formed to bless
The faithful with unfading loveliness,
(So feigns the Prophet of the Arab land),—
Near me a shape of wondrous beauty stand !
Blue were the robes around her limbs that flowed,
And blue the lustre in her eyes that glowed,
The bright locks floating from her forehead pale
Waved on the silvery whiteness of her veil :
(Such as on some high-favoured bard of eld
The Muse hath smiled :)—and in her hand she held
A harp of gold, while, as her words began,
Along the quivering wires soft murmurs ran—
" *If such be thine*, come, touch the slightest string.
" And it will echo tones so ravishing
" That thou wilt deem to thy delighted ears
" Is given to list the music of the spheres !—
" *Else silent all !*"
I heard, nor answer'd but with tears.

Now every tufted brake is glad
  With Spring's young melody :
Lady ! ere yet the leaves shall fade,
  We know not " Who shall die."

Thou art passing from amongst us now,
  And sad in soul am I ;
For ere September's fruits shall glow,
  Love whispers—" Who shall die?"

I check the rising tears in vain,
  I dare not say—" Good-bye :"
Ah ! ere we welcome thee again,
  Sweet Lady, " Who shall die?"

The Arjoon's leaves, dark, glossy, green,
  With haughtier jambool vie :
But ere its purple flowers are seen,
  Those leaves and thou may die.*

Friends have we many in the grave,
  And some are smiling by :
Who goeth next, I idly crave,—
  " LORD JESUS, Is it I ?"

" Thy Will be done !"—Be this my prayer
  To Him who rules on high :
O could I hope to meet *thee* there,
  I care not " Who shall die."

---

* The *Arjuna*, or, " Iron Tree." The blue and purple flowers
cluster around the naked branches in February, March and April.

THE OLD MAN'S DAUGHTER.

THE summer sun was hotly shining,
I marked the ancient hawthorn joining
  The shadow of the church,
As listlessly I lay reclining
Where thick the ivy wreaths were twining
  Around the old grey porch.

Beneath its leaves the birds 'gan cower
From the hot sun's meridian power,
  The lambkins lay below ;
And youths and maidens, in that hour
Were merry in the garden bower
  Where rosy clusters blow.

And one, the merriest of them all,
Trilled out a simple madrigal,
  In mere disport of heart :—
The song in many a dying fall
Came wafted o'er the churchyard wall
  To where I lay apart.

It told of one in former day
Who died of grief, and now she lay
  Beneath the sod hard by :—
But little recked that lady gay,
And oft the mournful tale would stay
  To laugh out openly.

Yet never mortal maiden smiled
With looks more lovely or more mild
  Than buried Lilian ;—
For I had heard, while yet a child,
How oft her winning ways beguiled
  Her sire, a grey-haired man.

37   D

Her mother died to give her birth,
And all she knew of love on earth
  Was centred in that sire ;
And she would lead the Old Man forth,
Or cheer him with her childish mirth
  Beside his lonely fire.

Nor scarce repined he at his lot,
Tho' now his long-loved wife was not,
  When in the sunny hours
He sat without their lowly cot,
While Lilian in the garden-plot
  Betrimmed the drooping flowers.

At morn the song of earliest bird
The light dreams of the maiden stirred :
  And still at evening's close,
The village maidens have averred,
Their solitary hymn was heard
  Or ere they sought repose.

One eve they listened for the sound,
But all was strangely quiet round,
  When hark ! a shriek of dread
Broke sudden on the hush profound :—
They entered, and the girl was found
Lifeless, her white arms closely wound
  Around her father dead.

THE THIRTIETH OF JANUARY.

THE Soldier,* ere he signs the stern decree,
Seeks Heaven's high Will full three hours on his knee
Calm as a saint, the Martyr Monarch lays
His head upon the block, and meekly prays :—
Now this, now that, with wondering doubt I scan :—·
How dark a mystery is man to man !

{

---

*Colonel Hutchinson.

D 2

SONNETS ON THE POETS.

I.—COWLEY.

My desire has been for some years past, and does still vehemently continue, to retire myself to some of our American Plantations, not to seek for gold, or to enrich myself with the traffic of those parts, but to forsake this world for ever, with all the vanities and vexations of it, and to bury myself there in some obscure retreat; but not without the consolation of Letters and Philosophy,—*Oblitusque meorum obliviscendus et illis.*"—COWLEY'S *Preface.*

I.

If genial suns or fragrant glooms can please,
Haste, mount the vessel, guide the flying sail ;
Where coral rocks bestud the southern seas,
Point the bold prow, and catch the balmy gale!
Where with bright green primæval forests glow,
Where the high arch of glittering mountains bends
And Nature in her broidered vales below,
Unstained by Art, her peaceful children tends.
Such, O Tahiti ! such thy golden clime,
Thy blue horizon, and thy laughing skies ;
So rove thy sons beneath their palms sublime
That in still air unmoved, majestic rise.
Their flexile limbs the feathery dancers bend,
Or in the glassy deep the divers smooth descend.

II.

Happy ! for there the cool banana's shade
Its ample roof and clustering fruit bestows :
For them the coco lifts its spiry head,
In whose full cup a guiltless vintage flows.
Ah ! bowers of bliss, where oft the glancing sun
Has viewed the sportive theft, the pleasing wile,
And the clear streams that gently murmuring run,
Heard many a vow, reflected many a smile.

Isles of delight ! retreats from toiling thought !
How sweet to lay the weary frame along,
And (what " the melancholy Cowley "* sought)
Pour in such glens some tender, serious song ;—
Sweet in your shades to slumber life away,
Or, like the pebbly current, murmuring stray.

III.

And is *this all ?*—for *this* was Being given—
To glades and glooms and solitudes to run ?
For *this* hath Man received the seal of heaven—
To sigh in shades, or batten in the sun ?
For *this* (O dead to Virtue, Genius, Fame !)
The polished walks of social life resigned ?
Quenched the deep blushes of indignant shame,—
Each energy that wakes the manly mind ?
Cowley ! I mourn (if such thy strange desire),
I mourn that Melancholy's cherished views,
Should in the museful mind sad shapes inspire,
Coloring each form with Spleen's unreal hues ;
That Love of Song should lull the studious breast
In sullen apathy and sordid rest !

2.—Milton.

A higher eloquence, a holier song,
With all the Patriot's burning passion fraught ,
Milton ! in thee to worthier action wrought,
Wise by the wise esteemed amid the throng—
Milton the friend of Cromwell—him who, strong
In conscious truth, thro' shame and glory sought
To win our land to freedom ; nor for naught
Waged he stern war against opposing wrong,
But in the depths of *thy* calm council laid
The firm foundation of our liberties.—

---

*" In a deep vision's intellectual scene,
Beneath a bower for sorrow made,
The uncomfortable shade
Of the black yew's unlucky green,
Mixed with the mournful willow's careful grey,
Where reverend Cam cuts out his famous way,
The Melancholy Cowley lay."
The Complaint.

And when night fell around thee, in the shade
Of blindness, want, and bad men's calumnies,
Thy soul unto itself an Eden made,
And heard the VOICE OF GOD among the trees.

3.—SOUTHEY.

Whether in thy hot youth, when fancy drew
To where soft streams of Susquehana wind,
Where man is ever just and woman kind ;—
Vain dream! yet, like a solar beam, it threw
Its spectrum on the Poet's inward view,
And hope was high in some far spot to find
The fair perfection mirrored on his mind :
(O ever lover of the good and true !)
Whether in thy calm manhood—calm, not cold,
With thy large knowledge and thy curious lore,
Still studious of the tales and songs of old,
Till the brain reeled beneath the gathered store—
Southey ! I love thee—love not only *thee*,
But thy wise prose and wondrous poesy.

4.—E. B. BROWNING.

A PEERLESS poësy—as pure a mind
As e'er informed a mortal minstrel's breast,
By genius, taste, and lettered lore refined,
Large glowing thoughts in gorgeous language drest,
These were thy praises : what remains behind ?
A sense that woman's weakness is her power,
A heart to pity and to love inclined ;
A smile, a tear—sweet woman's sweetest dower ;
The brain-lit fancy, and the heart divine :
O, who can read, and doubt that these were thine ?
Sweet was the music of her voice on earth :
Deem not its tone hath died with the departed :
Ah no ! it hastens to a better birth :
Be hope in sorrow *his*—the solitary-hearted !
                                                    August, 1861.

VEIL thy fair face in clouds, neglected Spring !
  Be hushed the voice of birds in every dale !
  Only the melancholy nightingale
Her sweetest and her saddest song let sing,
All night, o'er her departed rival's urn !—
  Daughters of England, ye take up the wail !
And ye who marked her matron cheek grow pale,
And her eye dim, daughters of Erin, mourn !
  If ever pure and gentle thoughts had birth
Within your hearts to Hemans' lay resigned,
  If ever ye have left the haunts of mirth
With her to sigh o'er suffering, sainted worth :
For she is gone,—and hath not left behind
  A higher or a holier name on earth.

6.—CHARLES LAMB.†

LONG time the Poet lived of life a-weary,
  All, all were gone, the "old familiar faces,"
  And of its whilom loveliness no traces
Lit the lone earth : with full heart sad and dreary
He sought his friends, but empty were their places.
  "Where now," he cried, "the *Ancient Marinere ?* He
  "Sleeps with the dead in Christ : time's haltless
    race is
"Run out with him whose voice was like a spell.
  "And where art thou, keen-thoughted laughter-
    flinger,

---

* Died in Dublin, 16th May, 1835.

† See Lamb's original verses, "The Old Familiar Faces," and his inimitable "Essays of Elia." He died 27th December, 1834.
  The "pensive gentility of Samuel Salt," eulogised in the Essay entitled "Old Benchers," was a relative of the present Sonneteer. Lamb's parents were servants to him, and contrived to scrape together no small fortune out of their "indolent and procrastinating" master. Charles was sent to Christ's Hospital, and afterwards put in business by Mr. Salt. In the third Essay, speaking of himself in the third person, he says,—"his patron lived *in a manner* under the paternal roof"—which, being interpreted, is—his parents lived in his patron's kitchen ! In that kitchen occurred the awful event which first betrayed the taint of hereditary insanity in Mary Lamb, and darkened her and her brother's remaining years. *Lovel,* spoken of in the "Old Benchers," is *Lamb,* the poet's father, and Mr. Salt's *valet.* The "narratives of Elia" are, verily and confessedly, "but shadows of fact—verisimilitudes, not verities."

" *Hazlitt*, my heart's own brother ?—O, farewell !
  " Vainly I seek ye : Death's effacing finger
 " Hath swept ye one by one : each hallow'd spirit
 " Hath gone the land of life and love to herit,
    " Hark ! they are calling—doth *Elia* linger ?"

7.—KEATS.[*]

SPIRIT, erewhile who dwelt our haunts among !
  Is thy name *writ in water ?*—Yea, it gleams
  In starry characters upon the streams
That gush eternal from the Fount of Song !
Thy years and thoughts were mine ; and gazing long
  Upon thy large, dark, melancholy eye,
  Methought it were a pleasant thing to lie
With thee beneath the *daisied sod*, where wrong
  And wretchedness and guilt are all forgot.
Holy, for ever holy be the place,
Where sleep the gentlest pair of bardic race,
Lovely in life, in death divided not !
O might I gaze one moment on that spot,
Peace for the dead implore, and for the dying, grace !

8.—SHELLEY.[†]

THE very soul of most sweet Poesy !—
  Like thine own Skylark, it was thine to fling
(Topping his notes with thy sweet minstrelsy)
  Wild music round thee.   Who like thee could sing
Ideal beauty in Ianthe's lay ?
Who tell like thee how in a garden grew
  That fair and delicately fashioned flower,
  Fed by " the young winds," fading in an hour,[‡]
The Poet's day-dream, and his emblem too !—
So fair, so sensitive, so from our view
Faded thy spirit's loveliness away.

---

[*] On his death-bed, the author of "Hyperion" said he "seemed
to feel the daisies growing over him."   If any epitaph were put
over his grave, he wished it to consist of these words only:—"Here
lies one whose name was writ in water." He and his friend Shelley,
who sang the dirge of Keats in that peerless "Adonais," sleep side
by side in the romantic English burying-ground at Rome.

[†] Drowned off the coast of Tuscany, 8th July, 1822.

[‡] The Sensitive Plant.

44

Alas ! Life's better lore he never knew,
But, maddened by the world's base scorn and
wrong,
Blasphemed the Power that gave the glorious gift of
Song.

9.—BYRON.*

FROM thee, fair Greece ! began the mourning strain ;
Soft as the Melody of Soul at first,
Then into one wild piercing shriek it burst,
As if the Muse had crashed the chords in twain,
That mortal hand might never string again :—
' Twas Genius wailing for her BYRON dead !
Aye, weep for *him* who tears of anguish shed
For thee on Marathon's immortal plain :
Thy land, fair Greece, he fondly, madly loved—
Thy ruined altars, desecrated fanes :
That love his song, his death, how deeply proved !
Great Bard ! while Liberty or Life remains,
Greece in her heart shall shrine thy memory,
Land of "lost gods, " but not one god like thee !

---

* Died at Missalonghi, 1824.

ISOBEL'S CANARY.

When old Catullus sang of Lesbia's bird,
His soul was with *prophetic* impulse stirred,
For Lesbia, if you mark the letters well,
Is but the anagram of Isabel.
   Was a *Sparrow* all her bliss ?
   Far more beauteous bird is *this*,
      Shy Canary,
      Light and airy,
      Sweetly singing,
      Like bells ringing,
      Soft or shrilly,
      Trilly, trilly.
And her eyes so beaming bright,
Glancing like a flash of light,
Have pierced my heart :—but ah ! I cannot tell,
Was it the Bird ? or was it Isobel ?

SAN REMO.

THE MAID OF ODENWALD.*

Heard ye that cry ? the HUNTER's horn is out,
Thro' the wide valleys swelling !—lo where, driven
From their lone haunts, the wild beasts yelling fly
Thro' the dark forests, or, to madness roused,
Mid the hoarse torrent, than man's ruthless spear
Less fearful, plunge, while peals of laughter loud
Waken the ancient echoes of the hills !—
Why scour your proud steeds o'er the bleeding land,
Lords of Creation ! ye are felt a curse
Where'er ye go, and the poor trembling deer,
All stretched out on the earth in agony,
With her last sobs upbraids ye.—
                                        To our tale—
A tale of rural innocence and woe,
Of pastoral innocence and filial love,—
Of a fair girl, her father's sole support,
Who, when by Wirtemberg's imperious king,
Her aged sire was summoned to the chase,
Adventurous, in the hunter's garb disguised,
Left the green hills and vales of Odenwald,
To join the train of hardy mountaineers.
Weary and faint, with cold and hunger worn,
Home she returned, with fond impatience glowing
To meet her aged father once again.
Her cottage-home looked drear and desolate,
The garden-flowers were dead, and from the roof
No smoke curled upwards : twice did she essay
To call, but terror choked her utterance.
With sad foreboding and a tremulous hand,
She oped the latch—then with a wild shrill scream
Rushed madly forward : on the cold hearth-stone
There lay an old man wan and motionless,
Hollow his cheek and lustreless his eye :—
It was her Father—he had died of want !

---

* The story, here versified, may be found in "*Austria as it is.*"

47

" Was it for this, from year to year sustained
" By the poor pittance of my daily toil,
" Thou blest me, and I strove to comfort thee
" With the fond duties of a daughter's love ;
" Was it for this ?" the wretched girl exclaimed,
" Was it for *this*, with torturing anguish torn
" From thy endearing, agonizing clasp,
" Benumbed I laid me on the mountain's brow,
" Or bared my bosom to the wild-boar's fangs,
" That thou should'st die thus cruelly, and I—
" I be thy *murderess* !

                    " Farewell, earth and skies,
" Our daily walks, gay converse, mutual joys !—
" Oft would we gaze upon the fleecy clouds
" Chasing each other o'er the azure heavens ;
" Oft list with silent rapture as the wind
" Sighed thro' the wavy foliage of the trees ;
" Or trembling view the grandeur of the storm,
" When at lone midnight, thro' the haunted woods
" Swift traversing with music wild and shrill,
" Dark Rodenstein proclaimed the coming fight.*
" Scenes lost to me which thou no more may'st share,
" Alas ! our home was as a quiet nest
" Embosomed deeply in the shady nook
" Of some soft valley : but the spoiler came,
" And cold and cheerless is the house of Death !
" My frame grows weak : rise, gathering darkness, rise,
" Clouds, fold me round !—receive my fleeting spirit,
" O my dead Father !"—
                    These were her last words,
They made their graves together ; and the bat
Is the sole tenant of that ruined house

---

*The appearance of the knight Rodenstein, passing through the
midnight air with martial music, is held to be a presage of war in
many parts of Germany, and particularly in the beautiful vale of
Odenwald. (See Mrs. Heman's " Historic Scenes.")

48

INDIAN CAVES.

The giant works of ancient days,
That echoed once with Vishnu's praise,
Revered by pious Hindus yet
In Elephanta or Salsette,—
What though mis-shapen forms abound,
And horrid idols strew the ground,
Those mightiest works of mortal art,
   In terror grim or mural white,
To Faith sublimer thoughts impart,—
    'Tis darkness groping into light :
Myths of the True, and shadows of the Sun,
Fragments of being, mirroring The One!

POONA.

PAPA'S WELCOME TO HIS LITTLE GIRL.

Thou art come, sweet babe with the violet eyes,
   The light of our Indian dwelling,
And memory's tears will unbidden rise,
   But joy in our hearts is swelling.
Thou art come, thou art come, sweet flower of Ind,
   The exile's home adorning,
Beauty for ashes in thee we find,
   And the oil of joy for mourning.
Dear GOD ! we receive her a gift from Thee,
   As we read in Thy sacred pages,—
" Take this child, and nurse it for me,
   " And I will pay thee thy wages."
Hail, partner of many a moonlit walk
   (Hope whispers) in years to come,
When papa and his little girl will talk
   Of the dearly-loved at home :—
Of the bright-haired boy, thy first-born brother,
   (Ah me ! how our hearts were riven,
When we parted with that dear child !)—and the other
   In a happier home in Heaven.
Thou art come, sweet babe with the violet eyes,
   The light of our Indian dwelling,
And memory's tears will unbidden rise,
   But joy in our hearts is swelling.

POONA, *December*, 1847.

A BALLAD OF ORIGEN.

Now listen, L., unto my rhyme,
  A short and simple ditty,
Of one who dwelt in olden time
  Within a famous City.*
The man taught rhetoric for hire,
  One son his only joy,
Leonides was named the sire,
  And Origen the boy.

The neighbours they were heathen all,
  On idol—worship mad ;
This lad would still on JESUS call,
  And JESUS loved the lad.
In JESUS' words was all his mirth,
  At JESUS' woes he wept :—
A smile—it was not of this earth—
  Fell on him while he slept.

One night beside his little bed
  His father knelt to pray,
Then—bowing reverently his head—
  He kissed him where he lay.
" Now wherefore kiss the young boy's breast?
  " Thou fond and foolish father !
" The child thou so much worshippest,
  " Thyself should worship rather."

" Our Saviour said, ere he did part,"
  The old man answer'd well,
" That in each lowly loving heart
  " His Spirit aye should dwell.
" He passes by the proud and high
  " To rest Him where He pleases ;
" So when I kissed my gentle Boy,
  " I kissed the Home of JESUS."—

---

*Alexandria.

51

Thus Origen his course began,
  (CHRIST'S SPIRIT was his Teacher,)
And when he grew to be a man,
  Became a famous Preacher.
False friends and cruel foes withstood,
  (One day you'll read the story,)
At length he shed his Martyr-blood,
  And went to GOD in glory.

Give God, give God the glory,
Ye giant oaks and hoary !
From wind-swept harps of praise
Loud jubilations raise !—
Bow your heads, grey with time,
Chanting your hymns sublime,
Forests of Fontainebleau !
While the rapt bard below
 Thought with thought interweaves
Thick as the thousand leaves,
Thick as the boughs with boughs
Interlaced overhead,
Casting their grateful shade,
Cooling pale brows.—

Hark 'tis the note of storm !
Dark clouds the day deform :
Silent as voiceless thing,
Birds cleave the breathless air :
Nature stands shuddering,
Silent with wonder.
Hark ! how the forests shake !
Flashes the lightning glare,
Peals the dread thunder !—
Now let your voices wake,
Forests of Fontainebleau !
While the red lightnings glow,
Crashing above, below,
Rending asunder !

*　　*　　*　　*　　*

Now all is peace and calm :
Nature her healing balm
Breathes, and the earth's repose
Deeper and deeper grows.—

　　　　　　　　F.

The rillet's silver chiming
GOD'S loveliness is timing
To the deep musing mind.
There is not one among
The many-voicèd throng
Sweet birds of every kind,—
The chanting stream, the breathing wood,
The " still small voice " least understood,
But tells me GOD is good.
The tiniest grassy germ,
With dew beads glistening,
Which the pale earthern worm
Circles with coily ring ;
The subtle life that feeds
The leaf-paved arbour's weeds,
Whose clambering tendrils shoot
Through the gnarlèd root
Of the grey father-pine ;—
Will sweet remembrance yield
Of HIM whose eye benign
Smiled on the lilies of the field
In Holy Palestine.
It is but bend the eye of faith
On the green moss-beds underneath,
Yfleckèd with the purple jet
Of the low-flowering violet,
Or with curious glance to spell
The blue droop of the hyacinth's bell,
Ringing with the light minstrelsy
Of the fairy harper bee ;
And ye may almost deem ye hear
The long-lost voice of spirits dear
With plaintive accents chide your stay,
And call you from the world away.
It is but with a gentle tone,
When ye are in the woods alone,
To question those sweet oracles
That haunt old woodland shades and dells,—
And the lone spirit will reply
With a mysterious melody,—
Hallowed as those rare voices deep
That breathe upon us in our sleep,
Wafted from other worlds, where they
Who have put off this coil of clay.

54

From their own bowers of beauty sing,
In pity to the sorrowing.
It is but fix the burning eye
On the blue radiance of the sky,
Aye smiling, with so calm a smile,
On all man's weary worthless toil,—
The self-wrought griefs which have their birth
In the dishonoured sons of earth,
Their weal or woe,—and you may see,
If of the poet's soul ye be,
The type of an eternity,
Engraved by the Great Spirit's finger
Upon each gold-ensphered singer.
The storm, the calm, the forest's roar and lull,
You oaks that tower, this grass my feet have trod,
All are but symbols of The Beautiful,
And Beauty is the Sacrament of GOD.

FONTAINEBLEAU, 1877.

THE CHRIST-CHILD.

Heavy I closed mine eyes on this dim scene of change
    and of sadness,
The shadow of sleep came o'er me, and my soul sought
    the land of visions.
Was it a dream I saw ?—a young and beautiful mother
Lulling her first-born Son with the throbs of her yearn-
    ing bosom
Very fair was that Child, fairer than children of man-
    kind,
Many a tear-drop sparkled on the gold hair that
    gleamed on his forehead,
But they gushed not from *his* young spirit ; they were
    tears of a mother's affection :—
She was so happy and proud of that bright and radiant
    Being,
That her very pride and joy made her tremblingly think
    of the future.
I gazed on that wondrous Boy, and I knew that his
    destination
Was to wrench the tyrant's shackles from the writhing
    limbs of the poor man,
Beauty to give for ashes, and the oil of joy for mourning
Over the spirit of sadness the mantle of praise and
    thanksgiving,
" Glory to God in the highest and Peace to His
    reconciled creatures !"

HAGAR AND ISHMAEL.

" My Ishmael, my first born,
  " My beautiful and brave,
" Soon will thy fair and spotless form
  " Be cradled in the grave :
" Vainly I cry on Sarai's God
  " Thy sinless life to save.

" Thou wast the lightest-hearted child
  " E'er cheered a mother's woe,
" And gladness laughed in thy young eye,
  " So dim and soul-less now :
" But pale, pale is thy pain-worn cheek,
  " Death's dews are on thy brow.

" I see thy saddened looks betray
  " The grief thou will not tell ;
" All day I wander thro' the waste,
  " But find no cooling well :
" I cannot bear to look on thee,
  " For my fears I cannot quell.

" I thought to wipe each gushing tear
  " From off thy cheek so pale,
" To clasp thee to my yearning arms,
  " And hush thy boyish wail,
" To shield thee from the summer's heat,
  " And winter's icy gale.

" But, Oh ! I cannot bear to see
  " Thy wild and blood-tinged eye,
" I dread to list thy panting breath,
  " Thy weak and tremulous sigh :—
" My Ishmael, my first born,
  " I cannot see thee die !—

" Thou art passing now to realms above.
" While I alone am left,
" For I may know no other joy,
" Of all in thee bereft."
Then Hagar turned her from the boy,
Lift up her voice, and wept.

Faint as the soft harp's dying note,
She breathed her melting prayer,
When, like a falling Pleiad, brushed
A bright wing thro' the air,
And Hagar viewed with wondering eyes
A glorious spirit there !

He pointed to a lonely spot,—
A small and grassy ring,
Then touched it with his magic wand,
Forth gushed a bubbling spring,
And thro' the wilderness it passed
With a pleasant murmuring.

Joy, love, and gratitude awoke
In Hagar's heart the while,
When, as she laved her young boy's face,
He blessed her with a smile :—
So kindly looks of sympathy
All earthly ills beguile.

Thus Ishmael in the desert grew
Sustained by God's command ;
A leopard's skin his shoulders graced,
A bow and spear his hand ;—
The patriarch of the Arab tribe,
He trod the fiery sand.

LILLESHALL.

"EPHPHATHA!"—BE OPENED!

MARK vii. 31—37.

The deaf mute on MESSIAH gazeth
  With meek eye of expectant faith,
The while His face to heaven He raiseth,
  And "*Ephphatha!*" He sighing saith.

"*Be opened!*"—and with the word
  A power of healing virtue came;
The Saviour's gracious voice he heard,
  And blessed the gracious Saviour's name.

All Glory be to God above!
  "HE hath done all things well," they cry.
Yet while He works this work of love,
  Say, wherefore doth the Saviour "*sigh?*"

When the dark tomb gave up its dead,
  And Mary's heart laughed,—"*Jesus wept.*"
O'er Salem oft the tear He shed
  While Salem's careless daughters slept.

Alas! He knew 'twere vain to call
  On *spirits* dead their chains to break:—
He knew that Salem's towers must fall
  Ere Salem's daughters would awake.

To Him alone how many an ear
  Fast closed He knew: how many a tongue,
All voluble in words of jeer,
  Dumb only to salvation's song.

Then, Christian! if thy dearest LORD
  A "Man of Sorrows" still appears,
If "sighing" still He speaks the word,
  And still His path be wet with tears,—

O marvel not! but ask thee rather,
  When Jesus speaks, leaps up thine heart
To list the message of His Father,
  And in His praises bear thy part ?

" *Ephphatha !* "—O the joyful sound !
  Hear it, our souls ! and every voice
" *Ephphatha ! Ephphatha !*" resound,
  While thousand opening hearts rejoice.

" Ephphatha ! Ephphatha !" again
  The soft, sweet, evangelic cry !
" *Be open'd* O ye hearts of men !"
' Tis Jesus speaking from on high.

"IS IT WELL?"

2 KINGS iv. 26.

"*Is it well?*"—asked the prophet on Carmel's brow,
  As the lady of Shunem drew near ;
" Is it well with thy husband, thy child, and thee ? "—
  For he saw in her eye a tear.

"*It is well ?*"—the lady of Shunem replied :—
  The tear fell as the words she said,
For her child, a child of promise and prayer,
  In his chamber that hour lay dead.

With the rising sun that child had risen,
  His cheek it was bright as the morn,
All jocund he follow'd his father a-field,
  Where the reapers were reaping the corn.

The sun rose hot on the young boy's head,—
  " O Father ! my head ! my head !" was his cry ;
So his father bade, and they took him home
  On his mother's lap to lie.

He lay on his mother's lap till noon—
  At noon he was cold in death !
Yet the childless one still could say, " *All is well !*"
  " O woman ! great was thy faith !"

When the best-loved of earth are cut down in their prime,
  "*All is well*," be our satisfied word,—
" The LORD gave, and the LORD hath taken away,—
  " Blessed be the name of the LORD !

" *It is well!*"- -*all* is well with them that are gone,
   If their spirits to JESUS are fled ;
All is well, too, with us who yet linger behind,
   If we follow the steps of the dead.

" *It is well!*"—for all things that GOD doeth are well,
   His Name, and His Purpose. is LOVE :—
Be hallow'd His Name, and His Will be done,
   On Earth, as in Heaven above!

THE NIGHT BEFORE DEATH.*

Thy name, sweet BLANCHE, thy lily-loveliness,
And these unstained camellias, all express
The whiteness of thy spirit's virgin dress.
" Blest are the pure in heart," the Saviour said,
And in His name beside thy dying bed
I breathe a blessing on thy gentle head.

SAN REMO.

*From " BLANCHE," by the Author.

THE NIGHT AFTER DEATH.*

How beautiful she lay! no trace
Of pain upon the pale, sweet face.
In robes of virgin whiteness drest,
Her white hands crossed upon her breast ,
From her white neck a white cross hung,
White were the flowers around her flung,
And " she shall walk with Me in white,"
Saith Jesus, " in the realms of light."

SAN REMO .

---

* From " BLANCHE, or Behind the Veil."

A VISION OF BARDS.*

I had a vision of the BARDS sublime,
Who sang of things eterne in songs of time.
DANTE, first mortal he who dared to tread
The darksome circles of the guilty dead,
Who heard Francesca's melancholy tale;
With painful steps and slow essayed to scale
The abodes of Penance and the twilight skies;
Thence upwards—guided by the holy eyes
Of Beatrice, as I, sweet Blanche, by thine—
To Paradise and the Primal Light Divine.
But when our English MILTON's voice was heard,
Methought high heaven's seraphic choir was stirred
By that large melody and voice sonorous,
And angel harpers swelled the sounding chorus.
Not far from these a gentler form was seen,
SPENSER, who sang on earth the " Fairy Queen,"
In measures languid with their loaded sweets,
But still he walked apart and hugged the green retreats.
See COWPER next, all radiant with delight,
Despair's grim veil torn from his ravished sight,
The blameless bard, his earthly " *Task* " well done,
By Christ accepted as his Father's son,
He shares the high-sphered Milton's wreath in "*Paradise
        re-won.*"
With him there walked a meditative man,
Prophet and bard he seemed with eye to scan
The beauty and the grace which are the dower
Of lake and hill, and of the lowliest flower
Which nestles in their bosom—of the least
No less than of the greatest. " Nature's Priest."
Men called thee, WORDSWORTH, but thy soul adored
No meaner power than HIS whom Nature owns her
        LORD.

---

*From " BLANCHE," by the Author.

LINES WRITTEN IN A STAMP-ALBUM.

What is a " Stamp-Book ?" ZOE, learn
And *stamp* upon your mind :—
As often as these leaves you turn,
Some lessons in Geography,
And eke in Modern History,
In every page you find.
These Kings, and Queens, and Presidents,
Whose features here you view,
Are types of Isles and Continents,
Of kingdoms old and new :—
Alike the fate of *Stamp* and State,
For one is old and out of date,
Another new and strange.
But still we sing " God save our Queen !"
Long may her honoured head be seen !
Her empire never change !—
If knaves and fools essay to sever
The links which bind in friendship close
The Thistle, Shamrock, and the Rose,
We'll *stamp* them out for ever !
So still let us sing, Hip. Hip, Hip, Hurrah !
OLD ENGLAND FOR EVER ! and ERIN GO BRAGH !

SAN REMO, 1887.

T H E   E N D.

Derby, Leicester & Nottingham: Frank Murray.

www.ingramcontent.com/pod-product-compliance
Lightning Source LLC
Chambersburg PA
CBHW030020030726
47499CB00008B/3058